A project like this requires inspiration, support and assistance from many people and, in my case, lots of coffee. I've been very fortunate to have so many family members, friends and professional associates to motivate, educate and push me to complete my cricket

Thanks!

STACY
Your six simple words became the title of this book.
Without them, it would never have been written.

MARY PAGE and NEIL
Your professional and personal input was crucial to the final outcome.

ANNA
Thank you for test-reading my prototype to your little ones.
That moment is what motivated me to push through the final steps of this process.

A special thank you Susan, Kyle and Keaton and to the many friends and family members that took the time to read my story over the past few years and provided thoughts, ideas and feedback.
Your words and support helped to shape the final iteration that ended up on these pages.

PECULIAR *adjective* | pĭ-kyool-yer
Not ordinary or usual; odd, curious or strange,
something important or of special interest.

There's a CRICKET in my car

Words & Pictures
David B. Baker

While on a Sunday drive,
to see what I can see,
I came upon a sign,
swinging from a tree.
I pondered as I read it
and began to scratch my head.

"Welcome to Peculiar"
Yep! That's what it said.

In town I caught a red light,
then I heard a chirping noise,
growing ever louder,
I began to get annoyed.
The sound I seemed to recognize,
though usually at night.
I thought it might be near
but was keeping out of sight.

Drivers started honking,
"get moving" they demand.
I had to find the thing that's chirping,
I was sure they'd understand.
I put the car in park, and began to look around.
I'm getting so excited, let me tell you what I found...

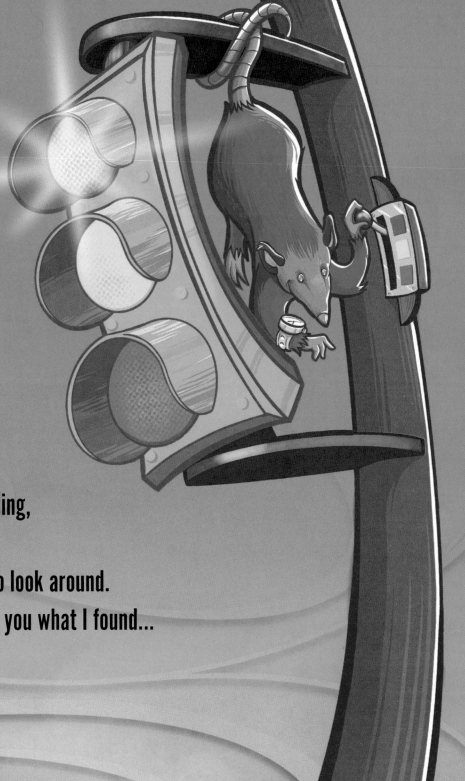

a spider cycling
in the street.

A monkey in the mirror,

a firefly with fuzzy feet!

A hamster dancing on a hippo,

a turkey roasting in a trunk.

I spy a bunny in a bonnet,

and she's skating with a skunk.

Near the mailbox stands a moose, sipping coffee with a crane.

A jovial giraffe
looks like he's balancing a drink.

Am I the only one who's seeing
all these crazy goings on?
I hear a person yelling,
"Would you please just move along!?"

If the cricket hadn't called to me, I'd just be on my way.
Instead I saw some silly things you don't see every day.
Take this as a lesson, there is something here to learn.
Excitement may be waiting, perhaps some fun at every turn.
So please don't be the one who's always in a rush.
If you overlook the little things
you'll miss out on so much....

Thank you for riding along with me!

If you had fun during your travels through my quaint little town,
I invite you to follow me on Facebook and Instagram for more fun
ways to enjoy your favorite characters from the town of Peculiar.

Cricket_In_My_Car

Cricket In My Car

Made in the USA
Columbia, SC
13 August 2021